NICK JR. The BACKYARDIGANS

Journey Around the World

by Sarah Albee
illustrated by The Artifact Group

Ready-to-Read

SIMON SPOTLIGHT / NICK JR.
New York   London   Toronto   Sydney

Based on the TV series *Nick Jr. The Backyardigans*™ as seen on Nick Jr.®

SIMON SPOTLIGHT
An imprint of Simon & Schuster Children's Publishing Division
1230 Avenue of the Americas, New York, New York 10020
© 2008 Viacom International Inc. All rights reserved.
NICK JR., *Nick Jr. The Backyardigans*, and all related titles, logos, and characters are trademarks
of Viacom International Inc. NELVANA™ Nelvana Limited. CORUS™ Corus Entertainment Inc.
All rights reserved, including the right of reproduction in whole or in part in any form.
SIMON SPOTLIGHT, READY-TO-READ, and colophon are registered trademarks of Simon & Schuster, Inc.
Manufactured in the United States of America
First Edition
2 4 6 8 10 9 7 5 3 1
Library of Congress Cataloging-in-Publication Data
Albee, Sarah. Journey around the world / by Sarah Albee. – 1st ed.
p. cm. – Ready-to-read
"Based on the TV series Nick Jr. The Backyardigans as seen on Nick Jr."
ISBN-13: 978-1-4169-5837-6
ISBN-10: 1-4169-5837-1
I. Backyardigans (Television program) II. Title.
PZ7.A3174Jou 2008
[E]–dc22
2007030301

"The 🌐 is flat!"
WORLD
said Queen 🦛.
TASHA
"The 🌐 is round!"
WORLD
said Explorer 🐻.
PABLO
"Prove it!" said Queen 🦛.
TASHA

"We will sail that way,"

said Explorer  .
UNIQUA

"The 🌑 is round so
WORLD

our ⛵ will end up back here.
SHIP

We will bring you  GIFTS

from around the WORLD."

Off went the brave explorers.

They stopped in Crete to eat.

In Crete they bought 🌾.

WHEAT

Next they stopped in Yemen.

In Yemen they each bought a .

LEMON

They stopped in Manila.

In Manila they found .

VANILLA

They stopped in Japan.

In Japan they bought

🍚 in a 🥣.
RICE   PAN

They sailed across the Pacific 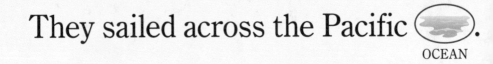.
OCEAN

They collected 🍲 in Peru.
STEW

They sailed on.

In New York they bought a .

FORK

They crossed the Atlantic .
OCEAN

In Cameroon they found a ___.
SPOON

Then the  sailed back.
SHIP

Queen TASHA was waiting.

Queen TASHA was worried.

"I guess they fell off of the edge

of the  ," she said.

WORLD

"We're back!" shouted

Explorer  .
PABLO

"The  **is** round!"
WORLD

said Explorer  .
AUSTIN

Queen  TASHA was surprised!

"Prove it!" she said.

They showed Queen  the

TASHA

, the , the ,

WHEAT   LEMONS   VANILLA

and all of the things

from around the .

WORLD

"The ⬤ is round!"
WORLD

said Queen 🦛.
TASHA

And they made a snack with

the food they brought back.